MW00893620

Olof and Lena Landström

Boo and Baa
in Windy Weather

Translated by Joan Sandin

R&S
BOOKS

Stockholm   New York   London   Adelaide   Toronto

Boo & Baa in Windy Weather

AB Rabén & Sjögren Bokförlag Stockholm

Translation copyright © 1996 by AB Rabén & Sjögren Bokförlag
All rights reserved
Originally published in Sweden by AB Rabén & Sjögren Bokförlag
under the title *Bu och Bä i blåsväder,* pictures and text copyright
© 1995 by Olof and Lena Landström
Library of Congress catalog card number: 96-68148
Printed in Italy
First edition, 1996

ISBN 91 29 63920 4

Boo and Baa are going shopping.
It's cold outside.

They take their sled.

"That was quick!" says Baa.
"Quick as a bunny," says Boo.

Boo and Baa buy carrots, potatoes, onions, bread, and a big cabbage.

Baa pays. Boo puts the groceries in the basket.

It starts to snow.

"We're going so slow," says Boo.
"Slow as a snail," says Baa.

Now the wind is blowing, too.

Boo and Baa pull their caps down
so they won't get snow in their eyes.

It's harder pushing uphill.

What now!?

"The cabbage!" shouts Baa.

"Catch it!" Boo yells.

"How do we get the cabbage out of the snowball?" asks Baa.
"Let's roll it home!" says Boo.

Boo and Baa start rolling the cabbage.
"What a good idea!" says Baa.

"Aren't we there soon?" asks Baa, panting.

"Funny how heavy it got," says Boo.

"It broke apart!" cries Baa.
"I'm hungry!" says Boo.

Boo and Baa make vegetable soup.
"It's nice to be inside," says Baa.
"Lucky, the snowball broke apart!" says Boo.